Welcome to Radiator Springs!

DISNEY PRESS
New York • Los Angeles

Lightning visits
Radiator Springs.

Lightning meets Flo. "Welcome to the café," says Flo.

Lightning meets Sally. "Welcome to the motel," says Sally.

Lightning meets Luigi.
"Welcome to the tire store,"
says Luigi.

Lightning meets Fillmore. "Welcome to the garden," says Fillmore.

Lightning meets Mater.
"Welcome to the desert,"
says Mater.

Lightning meets everyone. "Welcome to Radiator Springs